I Don't Want to Go

written by **Addie Meyer Sanders**

To Holden –
Have fun and
Go . . . .
♡ Addie Sanders
5-2013
⌣

illustrated by **Andrew Rowland**

Lobster Press ™

Try something new along with Joey!

Visit www.lobsterpress.com to learn the recipe for
"Grandpa and Joey's Super-Duper Secret Sauce." Yum!

This book is dedicated to Megan and Leyna, my newest grandchildren, and to children and grandparents everywhere.

Acknowledgments: For Dave and Phil for inspiration, for Meghan Nolan my expert editor, and for God, who is always there. – *Addie Meyer Sanders*

To my Mum and Dad. – *Andrew Rowland*

Published by Lobster Press™
1620 Sherbrooke Street West, Suites C & D
Montréal, Québec   H3H 1C9
Tel. (514) 904-1100 • Fax (514) 904-1101
www.lobsterpress.com

Publisher: Alison Fripp
Editors: Alison Fripp & Meghan Nolan
Editorial Assistants: Lindsay Cornish & Nisa Raizen-Miller
Graphic Design & Production: Tammy Desnoyers

Library and Archives Canada Cataloguing in Publication

Sanders, Addie Meyer
     I don't want to go / Addie Meyer Sanders ; illustrator: Andrew Rowland.

ISBN 978-1-897073-75-9 (bound).-- ISBN 978-1-897073-80-3 (bound; accompanied by recipe card novelty).

     I. Rowland, Andrew, 1962- II. Title.

PZ7.S236Id 2008   j813'.54   C2007-905420-X

Printed and bound in Singapore.

"Joey, is your bag packed?" Mom asked.
"Grandma and Grandpa are here. They're taking you to their house,
and you're going on the train. You'll have a wonderful time."

"I don't want to go,"
Joey said.

On the train, the conductor gave Joey an engineer's hat. *"Wheeww,"* the whistle screamed. "ALL ABOARD," the conductor shouted. *Chug*, the train lurched forward. *Clickety-clack*, the wheels hummed under Joey. Faster. Faster. *Clickety-clack, clickety-clack,* the train raced.

"Look," Joey said. "I can see the whole train."

When they arrived at Grandma and Grandpa's,
Grandma took Joey's hand.

"Joey, you have your own room. You have your own bed and
your own toys. And I know you and Dad like cereal before bed,
so we have that too."

"Thank you, Grandma," said Joey as he looked at his new room.

After breakfast the next day, Grandma said, "Today we're going food shopping."

"I don't want to go," Joey said.

But this supermarket trip was fun. Everyone knew Grandma. The deli man gave Joey a piece of cheese and the lady at the bakery gave him a cookie.

"Joey," Grandma said, "you can pick out five favorite foods."

"This is the biggest watermelon I ever saw. Can we get this one, Granny?" Joey asked.

It went in the basket. "I love grapes." In the basket they went.

"Do you like peanut butter, Granny?" Joey asked.

"It's my favorite snack on slices of green apples, yum. Let's get a big jar."

"Could we get some vanilla ice cream – and strawberries and blueberries to go on top?" Joey asked.

Grandma laughed. "That's six foods, Joey, but they all sound scrumptious! I think I'll throw in a few boxes of spaghetti too. Wait until you see how Grandpa fixes it."

The next morning, Grandpa said, "Today we're going fishing at the creek."

"I don't want to go," Joey said.

Down at the creek, Grandpa showed Joey how to hold his fishing rod. They waded into the water in high boots. Joey and Grandpa laughed as they watched the fish swim past their plastic lures.

When they got home, Grandma said, "Remember, this afternoon is Cousin Bill's birthday party. And you are invited."

"I don't want to go," Joey said.

Later at the party, Joey was given a treasure map and four "pirates" to work with. Joey and his group followed the map and found a treasure chest filled with clinking coins. The coins bought them a big dish of dirt and worms to eat. "Wow," Joey said. "Chocolate pudding, crumbled cookies, and gummy worms – this is my favorite dessert." Joey's dirt and worms disappeared in a flash.

Grandma woke Joey early the next day. "Today I volunteer at the museum. You can come with me."

"I don't want to go,"
Joey said.

At the museum, Joey loved the dinosaurs. He zoomed from one giant exhibit to the next. "I know them all," Joey said. "Here's the *Velociraptor* – he was a speedy killer. And that's a *Stegosaurus*."

"And here's the king, the *Tyrannosaurus rex*. Most people think he was from the Jurassic Period, but he was alive over one hundred million years later in the Cretaceous Period."

"Joey, I can't believe you know those big names and facts," Grandma said.

Later that day, after they got home, Grandpa said, "Let's go in the kitchen, Joey, and cook my special 'Super-Duper Secret Sauce.'"

"I don't want to go," Joey said.

Tomato smells soon filled the air. "Here, Joey, you can add the spices." Joey stood on the chair and stirred and stirred the big pot of sauce. "Ready for the secret, Joey? Promise not to tell?"

"I promise." Joey added the new ingredients and stirred and stirred.

That night, Joey finished three bowls of spaghetti covered with "Grandpa and Joey's Super-Duper Secret Sauce."

After dinner, Grandpa said, "Tonight we will sleep outside in a tent."

"I don't want to go," Joey said.

Grandpa made a big fire
and they toasted
marshmallows.

"I've never seen so many stars," Joey said.

"Look at those three stars in a row," Grandpa said.
"That's Orion's belt."

"The two stars above are his shoulders and the two below are his knees. He's the great warrior in the sky. He'll always be there for you, Joey."

"Just like you, Grandpa?"

"That's right, Joey. Just like me."

The next morning, Joey's parents arrived at Grandma and Grandpa's. "Get your bag, Joey. It's time to go home," Mom said.

"Already? I don't want to go!" Joey said.

"You can come back again," Dad said.

"Promise?" Joey asked. "Okay, then let's go!"